The Magic Show

Written by Jill Eggleton
Illustrated by Clive Taylor

Rigby

Tap!
Tap!
Tap!

"Look!
I have a frog."

Tap!
Tap!
Tap!

"Look!
I have a rabbit."

Tap!
Tap!
Tap!

"Look!
I have a chicken."

"Look!
I have a mouse."

Tap!
Tap!
Tap!

"Look!
I have a bird."